With love, for Aunt Pat and Uncle Dean, and our sparkling Kezar Lake —K. N.

For Stella, Sam, and Violet —D. M.

Farrar Straus Giroux Books for Young Readers
An imprint of Macmillan Publishing Group, LLC
120 Broadway, New York, NY 10271

Text copyright © 2019 by Kimberly Norman
Pictures copyright © 2019 by Daniel Miyares
All rights reserved
Color separations by Bright Arts (H.K.) Ltd.
Printed in China by Toppan Leefung Printing Ltd.,
Dongguan City, Guangdong Province
Designed by Monique Sterling
First edition, 2019
10 9 8 7 6 5 4 3 2 1
mackids.com

Library of Congress Cataloging-in-Publication Data

Names: Norman, Kimberly, author. | Miyares, Daniel, illustrator.
Title: Come next season / Kimberly Norman ; pictures by Daniel Miyares.
Description: First edition. | New York : Farrar Straus Giroux, 2019. |
    Summary: Celebrates the changing seasons as children swim in a lake in
    summer, collect pecans in autumn, play in snow in winter, and visit a farm
    in spring.
Identifiers: LCCN 2018004950 | ISBN 978-0-374-30598-7 (hardcover)
Subjects: | CYAC: Seasons—Fiction. | Play—Fiction. | Family life—Fiction.
Classification: LCC PZ7.N7846 Com 2019 | DDC [E]—dc23
LC record available at https://lccn.loc.gov/2018004950

Our books may be purchased in bulk for promotional, educational, or
business use. Please contact your local bookseller or the Macmillan
Corporate and Premium Sales Department at (800) 221-7945 ext. 5442
or by email at MacmillanSpecialMarkets@macmillan.com.

Come Next Season

Kim Norman

PICTURES BY Daniel Miyares

Farrar Straus Giroux
New York

Come summer,
we'll visit the lake.

When we spot a sparkle through the trees,
we'll race to the rope, bellowing,

"*Cannonbaaall!*"

before splashing into the clouds below.

Come summer,
we'll eat blueberries right off the bushes.

It will be our job to shuck the corn for supper.

We'll eat outside, smacking mosquitoes
between buttery bites.

Come summer,
we'll kick our sheets to the foot of our beds.
A fan will thrum, back and forth,
cooling our cheeks like the chilly wind *that will blow . . .*

come Fall.

Come fall,
we'll slam in and out of doors
until Mom says, "Stay in or out!"
We'll choose "out."

After a twirl on the tire,

we'll flop into fallen leaves,
scolded by squirrels,
until the trees stop twisting.

Come fall, we'll roar like hungry bears
and find pecans to fill our pockets.

Holding out our sweaters like aprons,
we'll fill them, too, until our waists
bulge, bumpy as bullfrogs.

Come fall,
when the colors have drained from the day,
we'll waddle inside to show Mom our fat fall harvest.

A tree will tap the window
with branchy fingers that will turn bony and bare....

come Winter.

Come winter,
when Mom calls, "Stay in or out!"
we'll choose "in."
Sorting puzzles on the carpet,
we'll look up when a TV voice says,
"Snow tomorrow!"
The next morning,
we'll choose "out" for the whole day.

Come winter,
after dinner and baths,
we'll scissor our legs to
warm the bedsheets.
We'll whisper memories of the day.

"Remember when the snowman's head fell off?"
"Remember the dog on the sled?"

Come winter,
as sleep closes in,

we'll think of the green shoots we found
poking through the snow.
Shoots that will grow into tall daffodils . . .

come Spring.

Come spring,
we'll visit Uncle Dean's farm.

Holding our noses, we'll admire a proud pig family.

"Be gentle," Uncle Dean will say as our fingers ruffle cheeping chicks.

Come spring,
Uncle Dean will scratch his head.

"I don't know what we're gonna do with all these pups.
Come next season, they'll be mighty big."
We'll look at Mom, *full of hope.*

Come spring,
on the ride home,
a fuzzy friend will nap between us.
We'll stroke her silky ears and say,
"You're going to love when we visit the lake . . .

come Summer."